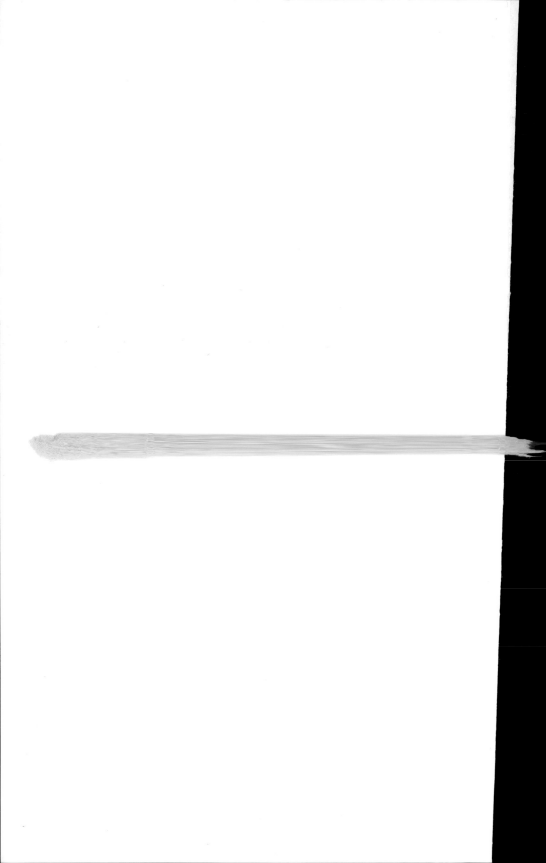

Potlatch Legends

Potlatch Legends

Written by
Tedi Brown
Patrick Moore

Cover design by Tedi Brown
Back page illustration by Patrick Moore
Sea Monster logo is the property of Alaska Totem Trading, Ketchikan, Alaska
All other illustrations by Patrick Moore
Photography by Tedi Brown
Edited by Bruce Wollam
Some of the ideas were stolen from the book, Princess Island Legends, written by our son, Kanoe Zantua.

Eagle

Raven

Smirk

Chapter 1:   The Legend Begins

I am the raven's messenger. I have come to tell the legends of these parts.

Thomas Talon is my name. They tell me I was named after a president. I've been on this earth so long that some people say I've lived forever. Maybe I have.

During the summer of 1937 I became the proud owner of a Ford pickup, a first in its class. The body was painted red and the fenders black on my '37 Ford, and it featured a rounded, low-to-the-ground look with fine horizontal bars in the convex front and hood side grilles and single steel bumpers of about six inches in width in both front and back. The spare tire was conveniently attached to the outside of the truck bed just behind the passenger door. The front grille was oval shaped, with so-called "bumble bee" featured headlights off to each side that looked sort of like eyeballs popping out from a too-tight necktie. On rough terrain, which included most of Ketchikan's roads, the truck bounced its occupants up and down like a mini-trampoline. But it was my truck, and that was all that mattered.

I considered it quite a feat to be able to
drive safely to my fishing town of
Ketchikan, which was ten miles south from
where I needed to launch my boat at the
"Forgotten Village." Approaching the dock
house in my Ford, I spotted the weathered
machine shop that specialized in propellers
and shafts for boats. As usual I was early,
"in with the tide and before sunrise" as they
say. The machine shop opened at 7:00 a.m.,
as it did every morning, so I had some time
to kill.

Sitting on the tailgate of my Ford, watching
the morning sun break over the
mountainside, its rays glistening like fine
gemstones as they hit the channel, I focused
my attention on Creek Street. Creek Street
was actually a boardwalk, not a road. It
appeared to almost hang over the creek
through part of the town for a couple of
blocks. During certain times of the year
when the pink salmon were running, you
could lean over a railing and see thousands
of the creatures becoming one with the
creek as they tried to make their way
upstream to spawn.

The boardwalk was crammed tightly with brightly-colored houses of red, green, and blue against the rocky cliff behind them. Amongst these houses were several lively bars, a dance club, and gambling joints to take the fishermen's pay. Dolly's house, with it's ladies of the night, was there, too, and its workers siphoned away any remaining fishermen's wages in the business of pleasure.

But, this early in the morning, no one was on the boardwalk. Only a few squawking seagulls sat on the pier at the end of the creek. The gulls were being watched anxiously by a sickly-looking, feral calico cat that seemed to be envious of their ability to dive into the water and rise up with herring in their mouths. I laughed to myself because I knew that that cat had no chance against the gulls.

As I looked to the right I noticed an unusual sight. Parked halfway up on the boardwalk was a gleaming red '32 Chrysler convertible with its top down. The '32 cost a lot more than my pickup, so I reasoned that the past year must have been good for Dolly's house. The car would normally have been covered by a canvas tarp to keep out Ketchikan's torrential rains, but this morning it just sat there sparkling.

Suddenly, the machine shop door swung open and banged against the rusty tin siding of the sloping building that was much in need of repair. There stood a short, bald mechanic with a single caterpillar eyebrow above mischievous brown eyes. He was dressed in greasy overalls and greasier boots, and he wore a grin as big as his protruding belly as he held a 60-pound boat propeller. He had been watching me from his grit-splattered window that was just above the flathead Ford engine he was working on.

"Where d'ya want it?" he mumbled.

Before I could reply he saw my truck, walked over to it, and not-so-gently dropped the propeller with a thud on the pickup bed. After settling the bill with him, I began to tie down the prop with donated old ropes for the ten-mile journey back.

With the prop secured, I began my drive down Main Street. This may not sound like much to the uninitiated, but it was always a challenge. As I rolled the tires forward, the boards underneath them made a snapping sound as they overlapped and ground against each other. I feared the wood would splinter and stick right up though the rubber tires, leaving me in a fix. The street was constructed with 120-foot pilings placed into solid bedrock underneath the salt water. It had to make way for the low and high tides which took place every six hours. The tides would vary from three to twenty two feet. It was on top of the pilings that the townspeople built a street made of narrow boards, which let me know about their existence with a clattering noise underneath my wheels. During those high tides I needed to turn on the windshield wiper to brush off the salt water that sprayed so high through the boards that it fell in a soft spray on my truck. It was like a gentle mist on a dry day which, in a town that averaged over

twelve feet, not inches, of rain annually, was
a rare event.

Up ahead was a one-way bridge. I pulled
aside as I saw cars moving toward me. The
first to cross was a silver '32 Packard. I had
seen it parked by the fish cannery owner's
house up the hill. I loved the rumble seat
that I'd seen his children riding in during
dry weather, which meant not very often.

The second car coming across the rickety
bridge was different still, truly a strange one
for Alaska, a '29 Chandler. I heard the
Chicago gangsters used them for high speed
getaways. They could easily outrun police
paddy wagons at 125 miles per hour. But on
this day they were lucky if the car hit 15 on
the uneven boardwalk, not that they needed
that kind of speed on a slatted run with the
creek and Ketchikan and the clear sky
above.

Then it was my turn on the bridge. Awaiting
on the other side was the only town taxi.

The plume of steam gently rose from its engine powered by a kerosene burner. I'd seen it at night where the burner would flood momentarily, shooting bright orange flames out from the sides of the hood and underneath the front wheel well as if it were the devil's ride. This Stanley Steamer had a momentary flash as it traveled silently, waiting to surprise another newcomer with a blast of fire as it sneaked along the drive.

Canneries were sited on each side of the boardwalk. You could smell them as you approached, plus the eagles and seagulls circling overhead provided clues of fish processing if your sense of smell was awry. Fish supply outlets stocked full of goods for the fishing season also sat on either side of the narrow lane. They were all built on stilts over the ocean water just the same as the town was.

I drove up the winding hillside that had been dynamited out 200 feet above sea level, which gave a perfect view of fishing vessels below. Those one-lung engines powering boats that were 30 to 60 feet long could be heard from quite a ways off. I stopped to marvel at the puffing from their chimney stacks as the smoke rose the same way it did on the Stanley Steamer.

This morning was a little different because there was an aura of excitement aboard the fishing boats. The cannery manager just announced the price of salmon had increased to eight cents a pound, which was quite a jump from last year's price of six cents.

Turning down the winding slatted road, I finally reached the dirt road where I was able to press my foot down on the accelerator, speeding along at 30 miles per hour on the open stretch clear up to the beach where I left my boat, the Alaskan Queen.

The Queen had a rounded belly like a whale's. Her deep keel was powered by a two-cylinder steam engine and wood-fired boiler, which could evaporate about two

hundred pounds of fresh water per hour.
The boat was only twenty-four feet long, but
between her cabin and deck she could hold
enough fuel for a ten-hour cruise.

I backed my truck down to the stern of the
boat, as close as I could get to it. As the
years were catching up with my physical
self (after all, I'm almost 87), I didn't want
to struggle with the heavy prop any more
than I had to. When I lowered the tailgate I
heard excited children's voices. I then
stopped what I was doing and walked over
the jagged rock outcropping to see the
beach. There I saw five children, three
boys and two girls, skipping smooth stones
across the calm water. I motioned for them
to come up and give me a hand. They
hurried up the bank like young goats,
meeting me at the truck.

"What do ya need?" the tallest boy asked.

I explained that the heavy prop was in the
back, and I told them that I needed help
carrying it to the boat. One of the girls,
trying to show off her strength for the boys,

along with two of the boys, picked up the prop as if it were an oversized clover leaf. They then bent down slightly as they slid it on the shaft with a clunking sound. I quickly spun on the washer and nut and put the cotter pin in place.

The Alaskan Queen was now ready for the water. I had about five hours to wait before high tide, but my friend at the neighboring shipyard agreed to come over in his Ford Model AA truck and push the boat closer to the rising tide. The AA was easy to spot with its dark green colored cab and natural wood sideboards surrounding its bed. Still, he had not yet arrived. Sitting on the tailgate, I was thanking the children for their assistance when Woody, a brown-haired boy with a bowl-shaped haircut and smudges on his nose and cheeks and lots of mud stains on his worn-out jeans, came over to ask me about a peculiar looking stone he had found on the beach.

"Do ya know what this is?" he asked with hopeful looking eyes.

The heavy rock looked like a mushroom. I explained, "It was a mallet used by the natives here over one hundred years ago. They pounded wedges with similar tools into fallen cedar trees to make canoes. Their canoes were between twelve and fifty-five feet long, made from just one tree. The larger canoes belonged to the chief's family, of course."

"This musta come in by a ship wrecked on the beach."

"No," I explained, "Where you found it is where it came from."

"How can that be?"

I then pointed to a dark green forest of spruce, hemlock, and cedar trees before us. Some of them had grown as tall as a hundred feet. This was once the site of a great village. As I pointed at the trees, I noticed three ravens fluttering about nervously, garbling sounds as if they thought that I was pointing at them.

Annie, a cute brown haired girl, who had
stood behind the others as they helped with
the propeller, couldn't withhold her
curiosity any longer as she asked, "What
was it like? What did they do there?"

I explained about the village life with its
seasonal celebrations of song, dances with
the musical percussion of hand held drums,
and feasts of salmon caught in the ocean not
far from where they were skipping stones. I
then told them that the natives also feasted
on the elusive halibut, as well as the deer
that they caught in the neighboring forest.
The chief would give away the abundance
of his wealth during this celebration, or
potlatch, that lasted several days. I then
pointed at the huge cedar trees leaning over
the waters' edge.

"See those trees? That's where I played
when I was a kid. My father and
Grandfather tied their canoes to a tree. I
would wait for my father to return from
fishing so I could hear the stories he and the
other villagers would tell upon their return."

The three ravens then flew very close,
landing on branches above our heads as if to
verify the stories that I thought about telling
the children.
Since time was on my hands waiting for the
tide to change, I pointed again at the large
cedar tree near the water.

"I'm going to tell you a story if you have a
little time," I said. The kids nodded almost
in unison and sat around in a semi-circle.

"I'm Thomas Talon. Some people think that
I'm old, but I like to think that I'm
experienced. This is where my tale started
almost a hundred years ago," I began:

I, Kundaka, was almost fifteen years old,
but time to me, as to my elders, is not long
or short; it is not relative in the sense that
most people have, though even in 1937 time
told in my bones. I could feel it then as I
feel it now. My elders, family and friends,
with me being the youngest, were beating
the drums and trying our best to follow the
village song and the dance steps in unison at
the potlatch on Chief Franklin's glorious

day.

The totems were standing tall for
generations to come, each to pass its
legends on to the newest of the clan. The
oldest one was propped up against the wall
of the chief's house, pushed there by the
force of the north wind. They were painted
in the colors of the earth: orange-yellow or
ochre, salmon red, the blackish charcoal
black, and turquoise blue, the color of the
sky.

I knew we had to be blessed when the older
men came over from their dancing. They
were led by the chief and were more
numerous than us boys who were nearly
adults. They paid tribute to the old totems,
the ones leaning against the chief's house.
They drew them in with their eyes, and they
touched them as they remembered their
stories.

The chief's daughter, Ya'el, came over to
watch with some of the women who were
about her age. She was obviously beautiful,
and all of the other young men knew this.
She had polished brown, almost copper-like,

skin that glowed. Her nearly black eyes fluttered as she watched the dance. Her long black hair flowed over her shoulders and across her chest where she would occasionally twist the ends unconsciously. The young men could look boldly at the sun, and they could show off their strength and courage for all its celebratory prowess, but none stood out in the eyes of Ya'el. She was like a goddess, and they were mere mortals.

And then it came, a call from somewhere, the depths of the inkiest seas, from the uncharted outer edge of nature itself. It was the great sound, the herald of the mightiest being. The sound rose rapidly in frequency over about a minute. It was so loud that it caused a flutter in everything that lived, and maybe even some things that were dead, in our village. It seemed to come from the very center of the great northern ocean without end, the one with lands of ice and snow, from a much greater distance than from my village to the town of Ketchikan.

The call, or sound, was a fitful cry, and it

was louder than anything anyone had ever heard. It was louder, my great grandfather said, than the time that he was a boy and heard the mountains thunder out their river of fire. It was greater than the fury of the waterfall, the massive moving river when it fell, the one that is in back of our island, according to the ones that have traveled there. Later, I would know it to be greater than the smoke-spouting ocean liners when they came to our part of the world.

When the elders discussed the mysterious sound, everyone agreed on one thing: the sound, in a way, was an answering call to the joy that we were celebrating. It was the response to our village's very own potlatch. Loud as it was, and brief, the noise had not even affected the tiniest baby. We waited to hear more, but there was nothing.

But on that day in the 1860's, we did not know that we had just had our first encounter with a creature that was magical, one that would befriend us, change our fortunes, and maybe even give mankind a parting goodbye. As the sun set on the day

of our great merrymaking feast, we
snuggled close to each other inside the big
tribal house and felt the warmth of the fires
lit to herald the close of the day.

After that day, life carried on for me much
the same as in all the years preceding this.
Well, maybe not exactly. There had been
that time when my mother and aunties had
rushed home with their cheeks flushed.
They had heard a mysterious roar echoing
off the mountain behind them.

"I don't know what it was, but it sure didn't
come from any man or animal I've ever
seen," said my mother.

Lately, I'd been watching people watching
me. Something strange and wonderful was
happening under my fifteen-year-old hands
and fingers. Miniature totem poles were
taking birth, some a foot long and not more
than two inches wide. They had faces and
bodies of birds, animals, and people we had
either seen or had heard about. There was
Chief Franklin and his wife, Pebbles. There
was their beautiful daughter, Ya'el. And

presiding over each of these was a keen-eyed eagle right on top.

I didn't try to make these totems in small scale; it just seemed to happen. I would chip away at a piece of cedar on the perimeter of our village, and then I would dream of what lay around me. My fingers would flutter in a frenzy with the carving tool my father had given me. I'd mix the colors from the colored earth, from ground stones near the creek, from plants, even from the wild berries we ate. I'd pound them all together and I'd check the grindstone until I got the hue of the massive old totems still propped up against the chief's house.

I was called to the edge of the forest, nearest the water, to help secure a cedar tree for a canoe. We stood under a particular cedar, judging its height and its girth. The most experienced hands set to, preparing to level it with fire set at the base of the trunk, assessing the best shape, how the seating was to be burnt out, and how wood was to be scraped out to make the paddles.

My oldest uncle, who traveled the furthest
seas, told me that we needed to make a
mallet to carve out the canoe. I must have
crawled on all fours near the stony shore
until I found one. I took it proudly to
Uncle, who thought that it would make a
good mallet, too, one that could be used
over the course of the next couple of
months.

Did we leave it behind or did it get lost in
the frenzied activity of canoe making? I
would never know the answer to that, but
what I do know now is that the stone had
become lost or left behind by accident after
the launching of this great canoe with the
eagle crest.

"Oh, no. What, what's that?" Uncle
whispered.

Uncle had reason to stop the canoe. He had
been on the ocean much of his life, and he
had never encountered such a sight now
rising before him. I saw it, too, and it didn't
at first make sense to me. It didn't belong to

any known whale, either from our time or from prehistory. It was the size of a whale's tail as it waved from side to side, collapsing back into the icy waters far below where we stood.

After what seemed like an eternity for us in our frozen running positions, Uncle and I were sprayed with tiny spindles of icy sea water that turned into an icy waterfall and lasted a good fifteen seconds or more. Later that day, when we were safely back home and we found our own voices, Uncle would tell me that that he had seen the sweet face of a woman in the gigantic whale tail. Still later, we would discuss what we could have seen. We spoke of it in whispers at first, with our friends and the elders openly skeptical at what we said we had seen. They were less so when they heard of our sighting from the group of canoe makers. The fact of the other worldly sound could not be disputed, since those in the village and beyond had heard it, too. Soon, it was all we could talk about.

Chapter 2: Eagle Boy

It was several months later after a dancing celebration that the tribe settled in for the night. They had no idea what was to come. They had only stored a small amount of fish, hardly enough for an entire winter. The hunters came down from the mountainside each night with little to show for their efforts. They followed the paths worn by the animals, checking under the huge yellow cedar trees for sleeping deer. On occasion they found a small deer, but nothing more. It seemed that the wolves had beaten them to it. Wolves had all night to prowl; hunters had only the shortness of day.

During that winter there was a huge storm. The eagle that usually perched itself on the highest branch of the tallest red cedar tree had come crashing down with the broken branch as it snapped off in the most violent windstorm that had ever swept through the village. Trees had blown down along the backdrop of the village, and now this eagle was upon the ground as well, tangled in the heavy branch that had it pinned.

I thought that the eagle had been killed because I didn't see any movement.

The eagle was huddled over in the corner by a stump. I saw where it had dragged itself from the branch, and where it had left a trail of feathers that it had sacrificed to set itself free. It was facing the moss-covered log. I poked it with a stick to make sure that it was alive and to stay away from its sharp talons in case it was. Well, as it turned out it was not only alive, but it also appeared to be very hungry. I ran up the muddy trail to the smokehouse. Inside, I reached over the coals, now barely warm from last night's fire, to snatch a small bit of salmon to feed the hurt eagle.

"There isn't much food, but this is an emergency," I said to the Smoke House walls.

I slipped back down the trail, clutching the salmon. I was sure the eagle would still be there. It didn't look like it was in any shape to fly. And there it was! Its eyes didn't look at me; it stared at the bright red morsel I held out in my hand. Its eyes seemed closed, yet it reached out and the salmon disappeared. That was it, then. I had an eagle to care for. Each day, I would slip into the smokehouse before anyone was awake to sneak a small bit of fish. It wasn't enough food to fill up the hungry eagle, but at least I could keep it alive. As each day passed it would come closer to me until we finally sat side by side.

The elders of the village noticed that I did not finish my food at the nightly gathering. One of the men followed me, staying some distance behind and stopping inside the shadows of the salmonberry bushes along the trails so I couldn't spot him.

I soon discovered I had been followed because when I returned after the feeding, the villagers began muttering under their breaths, "Eagle Boy, Eagle Boy." They were mocking my wastefulness. I didn't pay much attention to them, though, because I was determined to share my food with the injured eagle despite being hungry myself.

I continued my job of gathering fallen
hemlock branches for the fire along with the
driftwood that had come in with the high
tides. It was a daily task, sometimes taking
me a long way down the beach, but I always
scurried back in time to feed the eagle,
which was getting a little stronger every
day. This morning I actually saw it on a
branch above my head. I was happy to see
it there as the ground is no place for an
injured bird. There were too many mink and
martin looking for prey. Even if the eagle
found safety from them, there were still the
wolves who might catch its scent.

The snow was beginning to recede. It was
gone from the beach and the lowlands clear
up to the tree line. I saw the burgundy buds
forming on the stark branches of the alder
trees, a sure sign that spring was coming
and the cold nights would end. With the
change of the season, the village needed to
make a decision. When an area was lacking
food, the villagers would pack up to move
further up the waterway in search of better
foraging and fishing coupled with hunting
in the forest. There was no food to spare,

yet I, Eagle Boy, was giving it away.

Chief Franklin, who got his name from some tale that was told along the way about some creature or some human capturing light, confronted me the next morning.

"Have you been giving some of the village fish to this worthless eagle?" he said scornfully.

Speechless, I stood with my eyes cast down. I was not about to confront the most worthy of the villagers. But I knew secretly that I could not give up on my Only True Friend. I must continue feeding him as he now relied upon me. I stood there silently until the chief turned and walked away.

The next morning after the smaller rations of food were given out, I looked around to make sure no one followed me. I zigzagged along the edge of the trail going slightly inward where Eagle now awaited me. As he always did, he quickly left my hand empty of food where the salmon had been a second before. He had grown new feathers, deep

brown-colored ones where mottled brown
and white ones had been before. His head
was getting whiter, too, not just the brown
color of baby eagles. I figured he was now
about my age in eagle years. He was alert,
too; at that moment he was making his cool
stare directly toward the open area in front
of the tribal house, seemingly aware of the
upcoming decision.

Something restless began to happen in the
village. People were whispering. Chief
Franklin and the elders would meet in the
longhouse by themselves before the start of
the evening fire. They would decide
tonight.

After the elders had gathered in the tribal
house, I scooted underneath it with my
stomach tightly to the ground. I then
squirmed my way through the space
between the floorboards and the cold, damp
ground. I felt miserable.
The sand and ash from the floorboards stung
my eyes as I inched forward, straining to
hear their voices, hoping they did not hear
the beating of my heart.

No one was allowed to hear these secret talks, let alone me. When I got a chance to turn my body over, I had to cover my eyes with my hands because each time one of the elders began to speak, he would pound his talking stick on the floorboards to stop the whispering and muttering so as to get the others' full attention. Young people would oftentimes sneak through this same entry to listen to those above, later telling the rest of us of what they heard. But on this night I was alone; after all, I was the only one who fed an eagle.

After he ate, Chief Franklin stood with his ornately carved staff of an eagle, raven, and whale. He then rapped it on the floorboards.

I thought, "I hope no one else is beneath the floor getting this loose dirt in their eyes." My eyes began to burn from the ordeal, but I couldn't rub them because I didn't have much room to move.

Speaking of eyes, the chief's concerned eyes caught those who were looking at him straight on. Without much hesitation he

began, "We're too short of food at this
camp. We must move further north to get a
winter's supply of food stocked up.
Because we will return to this village
someday, we will leave one elder behind to
watch over it while we're gone."

The chief then went to the floorboard
behind him and lifted it up to pull out a
seasoned alder branch. He then snapped the
branch into different sizes before the elders,
who looked around the room at each other
because each one knew he or she would take
one of the pieces of twig to compare it with
the others. Their faces reddened from the
warm heat of the fire, as well as the
disturbing thought of staying behind.
Everyone knew that the elder with the
shortest piece would be left behind to fend
for himself or, heaven forbid, herself.

The chief put the broken sticks into one of
the woven berry baskets. Looking for
someone to pass it amongst the elders, he
chose the tallest one, an elder of about five
feet eight inches, the best fisherman in the
village, who took the basket and slowly
allowed each of the others to draw a stick.

Grandmother ended up with the shortest stick. She was the last to draw, and the stick was stuck sideways at the bottom of the basket. As the others realized it, they silently stood up and walked away, leaving her alone with her head held down to her chest and tears streaming down her cheeks. She was to stay behind with only the small amount of food left in the smokehouse. I couldn't believe that they would leave this old woman behind. How could she protect the village? After the chief and the elders left the smokehouse, I inched my way out from my hiding place. I had dirt and tree needles all over me, so I brushed myself off as best I could. I then went to see Grandmother. I put my arm around her to comfort her as she spoke.

"I am not crying for myself. I am crying for the children who are under my care. There are so many of them. Who will watch over them if I'm left behind?" Grandmother would not be consoled; she was too worried about the little ones.

Without a doubt as to what should be done,
I left the warmth of the fire to find Chief
Franklin, who was standing in front of a
group of villagers giving orders about
tomorrow's departure. He saw me coming
toward him down the path.

"Leave me behind instead of Grandmother
so she can tend to the children," I pleaded,
"I'm old enough to take care of myself."

Even though this was not the way it was
supposed to be done, Chief Franklin nodded
his head in agreement as he appeared to
stare straight through me. He was probably
relieved to be rid of his food-wasting
nephew.

Early the next morning, as everyone
gathered at the shore near the long canoes,
Chief Franklin announced, "I have decided
to leave Eagle Boy behind instead of his
grandmother so she can tend to the children.
It is final. Now, let's go."

With that, Grandmother again burst into
tears.

Chapter 3: Alone

After fully realizing what I had proposed about staying behind in the village while she left with the tribe, Grandmother felt better, knowing that she could continue to take care of the children. And me, I felt numb.

For the next few days there was much activity in the village. Normally when the tribe moved they would dismantle the tribal house, which was made with the force of gravity instead of pegs and fasteners. Pegs and fasteners weren't available to the tribe. Instead, builders could actually take off the final wall plank, and this made way for all of the other planks to follow. All that would remain was the outside wall posts and the huge inside logs crossing the entire length of the tribal house. But, this time the elders planned to return, so they left the tribal house intact. This was a good thing for me. Where else was I going to stay? The canoe makers were also relieved as they were already adjusting the weights in the canoes. The extra concern of moving the tribal house was now off of their minds.

I watched my friends, aunts, and uncles gather the cedar bark blankets. They placed them in the canoe to cover the woven baskets full of supplies already seated just off of the bottom of the canoe where the water splashed, out of the way of the paddles.

I thought that Grandmother was so kind to leave me her blankets. She was not worried about staying warm. She was clever because she knew that other villagers will lend her some of their blankets further up the channel.

I waved to my family and friends as they set off through the cold, calm waters. "I'll be okay," I yelled. I just knew that they would return in the fall. Grandmother knew that they wouldn't. Once again, she was able to foretell the future better than I could. I watched them on the horizon getting smaller and smaller as they headed out northeast. I didn't want to imagine what it would be like to be left alone, yet within the hour they were gone, and all I could see was the sea.

Slowly, I walked the path back up to the village. I kept looking back in hopes of seeing a glimpse of the villagers from higher ground. I saw clouds, the sun, water, rocks, and seagulls, but no sign of humans. I was alone with my thoughts, and I knew that I'd better get used to it.

As I approached the village everything seemed different now. It was so much quieter. All I heard was Eagle screeching as he rested in the tall hemlock tree overhead. "At least I have you," I yelled back at him.

I began gathering sticks and twigs for the night, reaching along the branches toward the trunks of the alder trees where I found the dry brittle mass of small twigs and moss that was so helpful in starting the fire. I wanted all of the help I could get that first night alone. It was me and no one else to keep the fire going, so I stacked the firewood next to the huge rock in the fire pit of the tribal house.

Next, I wanted to see what provisions the villagers had left for me. As I pulled up the

floorboards where each family had kept
their belongings, I found that I had enough
food for a week, and there under another
floorboard was my Uncle's favorite piece of
baleen. He couldn't have left it by accident.
I knew exactly what to make with balen, as
I had watched him make weapons for the
hunt many times before.

My youngest uncle was known as The Tall
One among the tribe. This was lucky for the
rest of the village because it was by his
height that they judged how long each of
their floor closets would be to keep their
baskets, extra clothes, fishing tackle, and
dancing regalia. Two of my other uncles,
The Bearded One, who was known for his
navigational and canoe repair skills, and
The Sea Skipper, who was known for
monitoring the fishing bait and catch, were
also very important within the tribe, but The
Tall One was the most revered.

Uncle was being helpful by leaving me the
baleen, but the lack of food worried me
nonetheless. I knew that the villagers were
in short supply, but they left just a week's

worth of food for me. The deer meat was used up long ago. It was difficult to find a deer nowadays as the roaming wolf pack was large, and each wolf could eat up to twenty deer a year just by itself. For humans, deer had become a delicacy.

At least they left me a little dried salmon, so I broke off a piece to share with my feathered friend. Eagle seemed to sense something; maybe that something was my loneliness. He then flew closer to me, his large wings moving the air with such force that I felt a gust of wind. I felt better just having him near me. Perched next to each other, we ate our fish in silence.

My mind began to race with questions about what I would do during daylight: "What about the nights? Would I stay warm? Would I be afraid?"

I pulled a few more dry sticks from under the salmonberry bushes that I found along the trail. Placing them on the small heap with the others, I looked around the room to find the spot where I would sleep. Chief

Franklin sometimes slept on a platform
above the fire area, so that looked like the
best spot to me. No wonder the chief slept
there. Looking up I could see through the
smoke hole, where later there would be
countless brilliant stars.

There in the corner, not far off from the
chief's sleeping area, was an oil lamp made
from a smooth flat stone with the center
pounded out to make a receptacle for oil. A
smaller rock was placed on top of the tightly
woven cedar bark that acted as its wick.
Next to the lamp sat two empty clay jugs.
There was no oil, hence no lamp to hold
back the darkness and whatever roamed in
it.

Then I had an idea. What if I could render
down oil from sharks like my uncles had
done. That way I could have light without
using too much of my valuable firewood. It
was time to put my thoughts into action; it
was time to fish for sharks.

I gathered up my fishing gear and grabbed
some rockfish bellies for bait. I already

knew where to catch sharks, which was in
the deep water just off of the big rocks north
of the village. Once I reached my spot, I
attached the bait to the deer bone hook and
tossed it in the water. Soon I felt the line
jerk, then jerk again, then pull hard. I
braced myself and felt my muscles tighten
as I slowly brought up the taught line. The
fish that swallowed my hook was strong and
fought like a halibut, but as soon as it broke
water I could see that it was exactly what I
had hoped for: a big shark. I loved the taste
of halibut, but today I needed sharks.

I managed to slide the shark up over a ledge
and into a shallow tide pool in behind the
rocks. I returned to shark fishing until I had
nine of them, which was more than enough
to make oil. The sharks were heavy, and I
had to transport them one by one back to the
village. Once I had my catch laid out before
me, I cut out the prized livers and took them
to the iron cauldron that sat in front of the
two ornately carved tribal houses close to
the sea. The livers were so slippery in my
hands that I had to make two trips. I then
found a tightly woven basket that I filled

with enough water from the creek to cover the livers. I also put some wood in a small pile to place under the cooking kettle.

I then began the chore of making the fire, which seemed to start up quickly when the others made it. This was not my normal job, and it was much more difficult than I imagined. I found a piece of iron ore that floated in stuck to a log. Luckily, one of the storage places under the floorboards contained some flint as well. I struck the flint and iron ore together over the dry moss and made sparks that fell upon the moss. It didn't ignite, so I tried harder. I struck the iron ore and the flint together, over and over, and sparks flew everywhere until one little spark started to smolder on the center part of the moss. I blew gently on that area until it burst into flames.

"Fire, fire," I said aloud. I was so proud of myself for creating fire. Taking no chances of losing it, I put more sticks on my fire until it was a small blaze. Once I was confident that the fire was going, I sat back and watched the livers cook until they were done. I was glad that the kettle was outside where the wind carried the wild smell away from where I was going to sleep. Once the livers were cooked, I boiled the rest of the sharks until the oil began to separate. Eventually I let the fire die down so the mixture would simmer out, leaving behind a pure, clear oil, which would be more than enough to fill the two clay jugs and keep a light for me during the eerie, coal-black winter nights.

Then it was time to grab Grandmother's blanket that she had woven from the cedar bark she had gathered off of the logs that had washed up on the beach years ago. Her blanket was soft and warm, so I drew it over me as I lay on Chief Franklin's floorboards.

Looking up through the smoke hole, I saw the most beautiful northern lights that were rare during a spring night, but welcome just the same. Tonight they were grand, with strips of red interlaced through the magnificent blue green dance of the night. Initially the light show was so bright that it seemed to be an extended day.

The night soon got colder and darker. The northern lights were special, but the sight of them made me feel even more alone. As I looked at the fire and the small amount of wood I had gathered, I realized that tomorrow I needed to get a lot more wood. This bundle tonight would last barely an hour. That was poor planning on my part. I separated the spruce cones that burned hot from the rest of the fire so I could quickly throw them on to boost the fire later.

As it got darker, I heard scratching on the walls of the tribal house. It was outside of my ring of fire and beyond what I could see in the shadows. I couldn't figure out what was making that sound, nor did I want to. It was too strange.

"What's going on?" I said. I could almost feel my heart pounding. Again I heard a gnawing, scratching sound outside … or was it inside? My hands and knees started to shake.

I then snapped out of my fear and put a couple of spruce cones on the fire so I could see. Mice! Mice were right there on the side wall. What kind of a man was I to be afraid of mice? The mice had sensed that the village was now empty. They began to take over their prize: the tribal house. I could see lots of them now as they scrambled up the wall. I wondered if they had been there all along. I had no fear of mice. Now that I knew what the sounds were on my first night, I fell into a dreamless, cozy sleep.

I slept through the entire night, waking to see the reddish light of day through the smoke hole. The chief definitely had a better sleeping area than I did, yet it was chilly so I quickly dropped to the floor. The morning fire needed to be attended, but there were only tiny coals and some ash left, so I put my folded blankets under my family's floorboards and set off in search of firewood.

I opened the door that faced the ocean,

thankful that we no longer had to turn our bodies sideways to go through the traditional hole that was in front of the tribal house. The hole was a good idea in the old days. If an intruder tried to come through the hole unannounced, the villagers inside could easily identify him and even conk him on the head if need be with the firewood that was always at the ready.

I looked toward the house near the beach where Grandmother and the aunties would tell the tales of the animals adorning the walls inside. There were Raven and Eagle, Thunderbird with Whale, and the Spirit Frog, among others. Each of the women would tell her rendition of the legend as she had heard it through the years. The stories came out similar, but boy, that one auntie really put a twist on them! She would look at each one of the young children in her care, point toward the deep carved panel on the front of the house, and begin her poetic story:

"Eagle flying high could not believe what he saw.

Bear had yet another salmon in his paw.
If Eagle had a human face as he soared down,
Then across it you would find a mighty large frown.
Don't you think you're being just a little bit greedy?
He said to Bear his eyes small and beady.
Be gone! Bear said with a very load roar.
And so he did. Eagle did soar.
So eat them all, I don't care.
Just see how well your tummy will fare.
Later that day Eagle flew back with crow.
They found bear asleep next to the river's flow.
His tummy was big. No, a better word's "huge."
Eagle laughed, you could tell he was amused.
You ate all the salmon you sleeping fool.
Now as you lie there with your tummy ache
You'll sleep all winter in a hibernate state.
Now, I can eat all I want
And laugh and tease, fly and taunt.
This is more than any eagle could ever want."

The children loved to hear the stories, and
each child learned them well, for the time
would come as adults that they would return
to this bear-protected house to tell the
legends themselves.

Eagle listened intently from the peak of the
roof where he sat today. This morning he
waited for me just a little closer to my level.
Seeing me, he came even closer, landing by
the glittering, gold-bearing quartz rock that
sat close to the front of the tribal house. He
was looking for food. I knew it! But I was
one step ahead of him this morning as I
reached behind my back to get the small
offering of the day. As I had little food, I
was thankful that he wasn't any bigger.

With the breakfast quickly over, I threw the
woven cedar bark twine over my back along
with some cedar rope that was left in the
smokehouse. I used the rope to bundle up
larger amounts of wood for the night's fire.
Down the bank, across the log with tiny
mountain ash trees growing up through the
sodden bark, I begin my search. Once to the
beach, I gathered cockles. Cockles are like

clams except so much sweeter. Anyway, they made excellent bait for the fish that I attempted to catch that afternoon.

As I tried to jump the muskeg area, my foot slipped back, sinking deep into the swampy bog, the wet area covered with moss so green you would think it was ground. Just then, I proved it wasn't. My foot was stuck, and I was just trying to grab the skunk cabbage with its large yellow leaves that felt like wax. Although the plant smelled like a skunk, the roots were edible. They weren't my favorite, but I was hungry. I didn't think I had to share them, anyway.

As I pulled my foot out, it made a sucking sound like the muck wanted to keep it. I then turned around to dig up the roots of the smaller and closer skunk cabbage, when I noticed that a large swath of ground lay open before me now as if some kind of creature had plowed through the entire ground, leaving only its deep tracks.

"I can't believe it! These are the biggest bear tracks I've ever seen," I said loud enough for ALL the creatures to hear me.

I placed my foot inside the track, which was at least two times the length of my foot. It surrounded my print and left wide spaces all around it. The marks of its claws showed deep in front of the pad. I had never known this kind of huge bear existed. I had heard about them only in stories, not in real life. On this tiny island, where it took five to six days to paddle around it and a week to walk through it, I had only seen black bears. I had heard the elders talk about unusual sightings of a brown bear that had swum the stretch of ocean water from the mainland of Alaska, but I'm not sure that they were as big as the track I saw. Maybe it was the monster bear that they talked about, the one that was among the largest meat-eating animals alive.

I snatched up any wood I could find as I quickly retraced my path back to the village, where I used to be safe. There were three inquisitive ravens watching me as they flew overhead. It was as if they had called the monster bear to come and get me. They seemed excited about my fright.

Gashing my knee as I moved up the bank, I
dove straight for the tribal house door. In
the process I scattered my wood across the
wooden floor, landing it close to the edge of
the fire pit where it belonged. That night I
would not let the fire go out.

Before I went to sleep I decided that I
should get off of the island for awhile. I'd
go fishing, which would get my mind off of
the bear. It wouldn't swim out as far as I
planned to go that day.

The villagers left me the small canoe that
was carved out by my grandfather. It could
possibly hold two people, and it would work
well for one, namely me. I pushed some
overgrown moss off of it and examined it
carefully for leaks or cracks. I ran to the
water with a basket, which I filled with
water to throw into the canoe to check for
leaks on the underside as it was too heavy to
roll over. There were no leaks. It was a
good canoe.

The tide was still half out, so it was easy to dig the surface of the wet sand to find the cockle shells. I smashed them on the rocks to expose the precious meat inside that would soon be bait. I then threw the bait into the canoe along with the fishing hooks made of iron and bone that were tied with cedar twine to the wooden pole.

I paddled the canoe out to some rock outcroppings in front of the village, keeping in mind the distance between me and whatever left those massive prints in the muskeg. I was sure to catch rockfish in the shallows that came up on the rock formation beneath the waves. The large fish, the halibut, were down deep, but they were harder to catch, as The Tall One knew.

I dropped my line over the side, letting it down ever slowly so as to not let it get tangled. There, right there, I got a strike! I pulled it rapidly to the surface because if I gave it any slack at all my catch would escape. I got the nice little rockfish with the sharp spines in the canoe, pushing it forward with the paddle so I didn't kick the spines with my bare feet, which I had done in the past and paid for with sharp pain.

I then heard the roar that echoed off of the mountainside. This time it sounded like a giant rockslide, but this was an animal from the sea. I didn't know what to think. Whatever made that horrific sound was somewhere close, and I prayed that it hadn't seen me.

It was time to go, so I paddled back to shore. The paddle surfaced the waves just as fast as I dipped it into the water. I pulled the canoe with all my might up the beach to keep it safe from the incoming tide.

I took my knife from the bottom of the canoe and filleted out the catch of the day. It was enough for the night's meal, and the carcass was more than enough for Eagle.

While I took my offering into the tribal house to cook over the fire, Eagle grabbed the carcass from the ground with his talons to soar to the nearest tree and light on his favorite eating branch. In so doing, he

crushed some of the backbone, which then
fell to the ground seemingly unnoticed. In
fact, though, the process was observed by
other predators that were lurking about,
waiting for darkness to arrive.

I began making the bow I had dreamed
about. It would be taller than me, stout,
ready for action in case the darkness did let
loose of its night creatures.

I tested the sinew that I found by the baleen.
It could only stand up to a few pulls as the
rope like line would slacken with every use.
I tied it securely around the tip of the baleen
until it was taunt. The baleen was difficult
to bend. I braced it against the wall using
my foot to secure the bottom of it as I pulled
it down slowly, over and over, until it had a
good curve to it. Then, I quickly tied the
line to the bottom of the bow.

Now, I had a fighting chance against
anything that might show up in the village.

Chapter 4: The Sea Monster

I gathered up the wood that I had dropped off at the tribal house, arranging it according to size, making sure that I had enough for kindling to start the blaze. Then I also made sure that I had enough of the larger, tighter wood to keep me warm through the night, provided that I woke up after a few hours to put some more on the fire.

To keep the sounds out, I propped a sturdy stick up against the door, securing the base next to an overly used floor closet where there was a gap just large enough to brace the stick. Anything that was inside would stay there, and anything outside would stay out or, at least, the stick would slow it down.

As it got dark I looked up through the smoke hole and watched the smoke curl through the air from my newly built fire. I imagined shapes in the smoke. I could see a fish, of course, because I was hungry, but then I saw a sea lion and then a monster. This imagining wasn't helping me. What I really needed to do was find out how and where to get more food.

I could get more cockles and clams, but I would have to eat them in a day or keep them in a tide pool so they couldn't get away. Instead, I'd use some of them for fishing. That always worked in the past. As I continued to plan for the next day, my eyelids started to get heavy, and I quickly fell asleep.

My dream of fishing was interrupted by a loud crashing noise. In a groggy state, I had trouble telling if the noise was coming from the end of the alders or on the beach. I sat up to listen. There it was again. The noise was even louder, and I was sure that it was coming from the empty food storage house. Was it a human? What about a bear? I wished that I could get rid of the penetrating smell that the wind caught through the cracks in the plank walls of the smokehouse, sending the signal of false hope of a food stash to the creatures of the night.

Then, I thought that I heard this "thing" outside. Did I make sounds in my sleep?

Did the animal smell me, too?

I got out of the blankets to stoke the fire. Maybe the fire would scare away whatever was out there. I stayed by the fire for a long time, straining my ears for any sound, but I heard nothing.

I stared at the door, certain that it would not hold. The door was stout, but my stick would break if someone or something pushing hard on the other side was determined to get in.

What was that? I watched a section of planks of the longhouse move in and out. Then, the planks moved further down the wall. In and out; in and out. What would make the walls do that? Why was this happening after everyone was gone?

There it went again! Particles of dust pushed from the moving planks joined the smoke from the fire reaching up to the smoke hole. I was certain that whatever was out there was huge! I heard it snort and then wheeze. Then I heard that low guttural sound, the gnashing of upper teeth crunching down against its lower teeth from its slobbering mouth.

"It's a BEAR!" I said to the mice that now hid in the walls. I was sure that it was bigger than any I'd ever seen. This was the kind that Uncle feared, the giant brown bear that could stand up to seven feet tall and weigh over a thousand pounds. I was beyond fear as the bear rammed up against the planks once again. It looked like they would cave in at any moment.

I could feel drips of fear falling on my arm from my forehead. The wet didn't even faze me, though, because I was so frightened. If the planks broke I had no escape from the razor sharp claws of this massive beast. I was shaking badly; I didn't want to end up as bear meat. I waited, hoping that the army of mice was silent. I could only hear the message "it's going to get me" in my head.

Then I heard the bear slowly move away. It was no longer batting the planks with its hairy paws. It was not coming closer to the

makeshift barrier of a door held closed by
my stick. It seemed to be going into the
muskeg area. I then heard a sound like it
was digging. In fact, it was digging up the
skunk cabbage.

I wasn't sure that I would go back to sleep
that night, but if I did I wanted to dream
about a better way to secure the door.
Again, I listened for the bear. Silence. I
kept the fire burning. A few mice were
scurrying about now.

These mice were different than any I had
ever seen. They all seemed to appear quite
fat, with light brown fur and white plump
bellies that were bordered by thin black
lines. Their tails were covered with short
brown fur which fluffed out into black
tassels at the ends.

The mice and I quickly became close
friends, sharing some food and the sleeping
area, which actually posed a bit of a
problem for I had to be very careful not to
roll over on one in the middle of the night.
My small friends would come close to the

fire at night to warm their little pink hands.
Of course, I would take advantage of this,
telling them of the day's adventures and the
legends of long ago. They didn't seem to
mind. One little mouse took a liking to me.
He was so friendly that I could hold him in
the palm of my hand as I told the stories. He
seemed warm and content to be there.

Late in the evening after I had made our
nighttime fire, the mice would come from
under the floor boards, their cheeks bulging
with the seeds they had brought for dinner.
They actually placed the seeds on a stone
close to the fire as if they were attempting to
warm them. Then they would choose a
small seed from the lot and nibble on it as
they faced the fire.
Truly they were my nighttime friends.

I woke up tired the next morning after
worrying about a possible encounter with a
bear. I looked at the stick bracing the door,
and I knew that the bear could have easily
broken in if it had wanted to. But it didn't,
and it was a new day.

Once outside, I scouted around until I saw
Eagle perched on the smokehouse at the end
of the trail. He screeched a warning to me.
I passed the Fog Woman totem on the way
to where he was sitting as I followed the
giant bear tracks that encircled the house
where abundant salmon had been kept in the
past. Because the fish smell was still strong
and inviting, the bear would no doubt
return. Why it didn't crash through the
smokehouse door last night I would never
know. I wondered, was Eagle guarding me
from this little house all night?

I then searched the village for any weapon
that I could use against the bear.
Chief Franklin might have left something in
his private dwelling behind the family
totem, so I looked there first. He did leave
some things all right. There was a mask he
used for dancing ceremonies with the frog
on its crest; Chief was of the Eagle Frog
clan. And the carving of Raven with the
Sun still held up the back wall. There were
also petrified clamshells heaped by the old
totem in the corner that he made years ago.
I only wished that he were there. Of course,

he wasn't, and there were no weapons.

I can still hear Chief Franklin's talk: "We live in a land of predators. We, too, are the predators. When the predators are in balance everything lives together in harmony. When the predators are imbalanced, then only the strongest survive."

At this point I decided to go fishing, not just for the food, but also to figure out my plight. The day was turning out to be mostly sunny and warm. The wind was calm and the water was smooth. Seeing this, I dragged a canoe to the water's edge, got in with my fishing gear, and set off past the seaweed-covered rocks that shone a bright gold color in the morning sunlight. "I'll grab some of that stuff for my dinner when I get back," I said to myself.

It didn't take long before I had paddled out far enough to see what I could catch. I attached a piece of cockle to my hook and threw it over the side. Soon I felt some action on my pole, which I jerked a little to set the hook, and I quickly brought in a spiny-backed rockfish, which I threw in the front of the canoe so I wouldn't step on it and feel a spine in one of my feet. One fish, then two, then six - it was a great catch for someone who was as hungry as I was. No doubt Eagle would like to share in the catch, too. Each fish met up with my heavy driftwood club so as not to get any ideas about flopping out of the canoe.

When I decided that I had caught enough fish for the day, I headed the canoe back toward the rocky beach to a spot that was just a little bit farther up and sandy, where I thought that I could easily pull my craft out of the water. I paddled a little and then a lot, but the current seemed odd. It kept pulling me backwards. Paddle forward, pull back. Paddle forward, pull back. I gained just a few feet, then I sensed something behind me. I thought that it might be a large piece of driftwood pushing the waves in a different direction.

Then I saw something bigger than a grizzly bear surface the water, its wake gushing sideways as it rose higher. I froze in fear. All I had was my club and my paddle to protect me from this sea creature, and they seemed useless in my hands. I yelled. I screamed. But the sea creature kept coming toward me. Its eye was as big as my head. It looked like a predator, and I felt like prey. I prayed I wasn't!

Below the stalking eyeball and protruding five feet or so in front of it was an enormous snout with two black holes at its top that snorted loudly and then spouted a gooey-looking liquid upward like a whale. And teeth - sharp and plentiful and big - seemed to drool a foamy substance as the creature looked in my direction. I thought that I was a dead man for sure. Then it looked away.

It held its ground, and I mine. I hesitated to look at it because I was so scared. But I had to look. The greenish-brown creature had a large appendage on the top of its head that curled like a scaly topknot. Giant, rigid fins, each separated by several feet, covered its spine. Hundreds, maybe thousands, of blood red, oblong scales covered its skin. I

couldn't see all of it, just its monstrous head and body that raised some fifty feet or more out of the water.

As I stared, the creature again turned its head my way. The bright sun created a strange black outline off of its dark red scales. I watched, frozen in place, as it's teeth parted further and further apart until it's mouth was wide open. The gaping cavern rose over me, quickly dipping downward to dump a catch of fish right in my lap. Its eye caught mine for just a moment before its gigantic body disappeared under the ocean. The fluke of its tail, which was at least 20 feet wide with those rigid scales attached on either side just before the fluke, was the last part to vanish into the Tongass Narrows.

"Whew," I said to myself. I couldn't believe that the creature had disappeared and I was still alive in my canoe surrounded by flopping fish. I sat there motionless, but then my canoe drifted backwards in the white capped current. I was being pulled again, so I started to paddle frantically.

Suddenly it jerked me again and I was being sucked into the path, or even the mouth, of the creature. I was within a foot as it began to rise out of the water. Its foul fish breath gagged me. Its green and yellow teeth, long and sharp, were within my reach, which meant that I was within their reach.

The side of my canoe now brushed against the sea monster. As I stuck out my left hand to push myself away from it and certain death, my hand and half of my arm sunk into a reddish slime that covered the monster's armor-like plates. My hand was just below its eye, and the eye was looking at me.

I then pushed hard against the sea monster's armor and my canoe slid away. For some reason the creature let me pass. As I continued to retreat, getting farther and farther away from what I was certain was my demise, I peered back and saw the beast looking at me. For some strange reason it appeared humored by my presence; I thought I saw it smile. I wondered if I was going mad, but then it made a noise that sounded like a hundred people laughing loudly at once. I yelled, but then I heard the noise again. It came from the deepest part of it's throat traveling up through the air until the winded sound echoed back from the side of the mountain behind me.

The voice didn't seem threatening to me, yet I wasn't going to stick around to see whether it was playing a joke or simply not hungry after heaving it's lunch on me. I paddled with a fury to put distance between myself and the sea monster. I was in a rapid retreat, and it seemed to be working. I looked back, and all I could see was water. As I paddled by the bay, I thought I saw a red tide. Was that caused by falling scales from the sea monster? I had trouble thinking because I was still scared. I didn't have trouble paddling with all my strength for the same reason; being frightened gave me unbelievable power.

I finally reached the safety of the beach and with it home. Exhausted, I dragged the canoe up the beach. It felt heavier and

heavier as I was getting calmer and calmer.
I secured it in its normal spot, and then I
turned to face the sea. I sat down, but I
couldn't stop looking and wondering.

Did the sea monster actually smile and
laugh at me? Was it just playing a game? It
had a chance to kill and eat me. Just like the
cockle was bait for the fish, I could have
been the sea monster's bait. But there I was,
back safe at home. "Eagle Boy, you're one
lucky man," I said to the mice in case they
were listening.

Did I miss something the elders said about
the sea monster? Maybe or maybe not, but
it didn't matter. I was alive and I needed to
get back to work.

I went about the task of filleting the
rockfish. This time I was careful to throw
the small scraps in the ocean, keeping all of
the white meat and the carcasses for Eagle.
I'd bury the extra ones in the sand, hoping
that the bear wouldn't smell them. I was
quite a distance from the longhouse so I
thought my burial spot would be okay.

That night there was a feast for two! As I prepared to carry the day's bounty up the path I heard the seagulls cry in unison. I looked to see them circle over the gushing, bubbling water beneath them, but I was petrified as I saw the sea monster's ugly head slowly rising up. I ran for the nearest large rock to find a hiding place.

With my back pushed tightly against the back of the rock, I listened to the gulls, the swoosh of water, and then something coming out of the water. I didn't move. I was barely breathing. I heard the water being shaken from the body of whatever it was that came upon land. I sneaked up to look over the rock but saw nothing.

When I turned around I saw not one but two giant wolves coming toward me. Were they after me? I didn't even hear their footsteps. They looked at one another as if they were trying to decide how to devour me. They were gigantic even with their soaked fur. The larger one stood close to 15 hands high at the tip of its backbone. It was bigger than

big, and the smaller one was huge, too. Had they just swum from the large island across the channel? Was that tainted blood across their backs? I closed my eyes as they came closer and closer. I held my breath and tried to play dead. It was too late to run. I could feel the rough pad of the bigger one's paw as it held it against my chest and breathed in my face. Ugh, that awful odor. It smelled like that putrid fish breath that I'd smelled earlier that day in the canoe.

I couldn't believe it, but I felt the heavy paw pull back from my chest and release me. As I opened my eyes I saw the last of the wolves' back feet and tails disappear over the rock. Just as soon as they had come they were gone. Their fast retreat blew the top of my hair in their wake like the wind from the ocean always ruffled the feathers of the ever present ravens in the trees.

Incredibly I was alone again. As I calmed down, I began to realize that this had been a day like no other. I had survived a grizzly bear, a sea monster, and wolves. It was then that I wondered if Eagle Boy was much more than just a name. After all, I had faced more than I should have three times in one day, and I was still alive and intact.

It had been three weeks since I had seen the bear, sea monster, and wolves. I began to gain more confidence. I searched the beaches for larger pieces of driftwood that I could carve into totems by the fire at night. I remembered the stories passed down to me by Grandmother and my aunties long ago. It was only right that I should carve the characters in the stories on a cedar tree for others to learn the legends.

The first totem that I would carve would be from the legend of Sea Woman. I felt very close to her now that I'd had my encounter with Sea Monster. Sea Woman's husband had gone fishing just as I had, but he didn't return. Weeks passed while she sat by the shore waiting for him. Finally she asked Owl to fly the skies in search of her husband. Owl had keen eyes, but he still hadn't seen a human before he reported back to Sea Woman. Perhaps her husband had gone to the world of the sea. Sea Woman sent a whale, Orca, to swim the ocean depths to find her love. But he, too, came back empty-handed.

Desperate to learn of her husband's fate, Sea Woman asked Raven to search the world over, to fly to every part of it, and bring him home. Raven came back the very next day. He told her that in the twilight he found her husband by a fire on a tiny island.

Later that day she was seen riding the back of Killer Whale with Owl and Raven flying overhead as she headed toward the sunset, out toward the island.

That would be my first totem. All I needed to do was transfer my thoughts and experiences into the wood.

Chapter 5: Wolves from the Deep

I had just awakened. I stayed covered under the woven blankets on the cool mid-summer morning as I watched the daylight through the smoke hole. As I began to look around the tribal house, I was awestruck each time I saw the Mother and Child panel that encompassed the whole north wall. Each hand-carved cedar plank represents the mother giving knowledge to her child. With the palms of her hands held high facing outward, the mother invites all who enter the longhouse to receive all the knowledge she has to offer. The child pictured on the panel below her feels protected. On the opposite wall was the massive Thunderbird, a symbol of power and strength, with its giant wings outstretched.

As much as I wanted to rest, look at carvings, and daydream, I knew that it was time to get up, so I pulled myself up from my warm bed and crossed the creaky wooden floor to take down the sturdy branch that I had found to secure the door. When I opened the door, I saw a familiar

sight waiting for me: my feathered friend.
Off I went to the beach where I had hidden
the rockfish carcasses. It was a good thing
Eagle didn't mind fish that was a few days
old. He would find me later on looking for
more firewood in the depths of the forest; I
had already used up the pieces I had found
along the banks.

"What's this?" I said, "This is a first."
Eagle came after me instead of eating the
rockfish. If he didn't want to eat, then we'd
go fishing instead.

As I headed down toward the beach, I began
to feel the presence of the two giant wolves
that I had seen on the day I encountered the
sea monster. I saw the bigger one coming
toward me first. Its fur was dripping as it
emerged from the sea. The smaller one,
obviously a female, was following behind
the male with what looked like a whale's
fluke close to its body. This didn't make
sense to me; I couldn't believe that a whale
would swim that close to shore. I worried
that the whale might try to maneuver the
wolves back out to deeper water and attack

them. But, the fluke soon disappeared under the surface of the shallow froth that was coming up to the beach.

The larger wolf made its way out of the water as the smaller one brushed its side, and both began to shake water everywhere as they moved their bodies back and forth, trying to rid themselves of the cold salt water. Strangely, I felt no threat or fear as they came nearer to me. Soon they were close enough that I could reach out and touch their vivid black and red scaled fur that was shining brightly in the sunlight.

Then the large wolf lowered its snout over my head, blowing hot salt water from its nostrils all over me. "At least it was salt water," I thought, "not the slime that the sea monster blew on me."

I pulled my hand back, and then for some reason I felt compelled to talk to the wolves. I explained in much detail why I was alone in the village, including the part about feeding Eagle. They seemed to listen. I wanted them to stay, so I said, "I have a

name. It's Kundaka, but the villagers call
me Eagle Boy. What are your names?"

Watching the large wolf circle me, I thought
I saw it smile. It was a smile formed from
its reddish black lips that pulled back up
into its cheeks. Actually, it looked like a
smirk, a wolf smirk.

"You've been smirking at me since the first
day I met you. I'll call you Smirk!"

The wolf behind Smirk seemed shy, yet
kind. She seemed to always be leaning on
Smirk.

"I'll call you the one that is shy. No, I'll call
you Shylean."

That same clever smile crept across Smirk's
face again when I said, "It's settled. I'll
call you Smirk and Shylean."

They stayed close by on the grassy knoll
just beyond where I was sitting and soaking
up the warm summer day between rain
showers. Then I saw the wolves' lips curl

back. This time it wasn't a smirk. At the same time I heard the crackling of twigs and the sound of pebbles being crushed from the weight of something heavy over by the tribal house with the four Thunderbirds carved on the front. Then ravens began to caw loudly, flying from branch to branch, one landing almost on top of the other to avoid the sharp branch broken off from last week's storm. I followed their intent look to see what all the commotion was about.

And there it was: brown and gigantic, at least a thousand pounds or more, mean and hungry looking. Then the sound "grrrrrahhh, grrrrrahhh" filled the air and silenced all of the other creatures. Maybe the largest bear on earth was coming out of my woods. These grizzly bears fear nothing as nothing has been able to stop them in their territory. I didn't stand a chance against this beast with the new stick that I thought was so stout. I had even fashioned a sharp stone to attach to the stick with more of the hemp rope that I had found washed up between two logs. Now my spear looked like a toy. I had to weigh my options quickly to escape the bear's fury. I could run to the ocean and dive under the cold, frothy waves, or try to outrun the bear in the forest. But I knew each choice would be futile. This was the end of Eagle Boy.

Right then the bear stood up. It was as tall as a man standing on another man's shoulders. It's body shook the ground as it fell back down. The smell of fish had brought it around, and it came toward me as if I were a large salmon. It waved its enormous head from side to side, its breath steaming from its mouth where white spit had formed. I could see the intensity in its dark eyes. It seemed crazed as it pushed its hind legs in the sand to start its lunge for me before I could turn to run to the sea. I reached for my bow, but I was too slow to aim my weapon.

I heard the bow snap part of the baleen as it ripped my skin through my shirt. I didn't feel any pain, though; I was too terrified. In one turn the bear threw the broken bow fifteen feet away from me. The impact had pushed me to the ground, where I was even more defenseless. I then tried crawling to the water.

I looked over my back to see Smirk jump in front of the bear. He was almost as big as the grizzly, and he was ready to fight. Shylean then jumped from the knoll. She sank her teeth into the bear's hind leg, but this made it furious and it smacked her with its giant paw. The force sent Shylean rolling and tumbling back to the knoll.

Smirk saw this action and quickly flew through the air, landing his sharp fangs and claws into the back of the bear's neck. He held on tightly as the bear tried to shake him off of its back. But Smirk held on tighter, only letting go for a split second to grab the underside of the bear's fat neck that was hidden behind its thick and coarse brown hair.

As I watched the fight I regained my senses. Standing up, I saw Smirk corral the monstrous grizzly bear and force it back down to the ground as he bit through the bear's throat until it lay motionless in a large puddle of blood not far from my useless bow. Some of Shylean's stained red scales that the bear had ripped off were also on the ground.

Soon after the battle ended Smirk loped toward the limping Shylean. They then went off together toward the ocean and disappeared by the rocks.

I stared at the bear until I was sure that it was dead, then got out my knife to skin it out for a blanket for warmth when the snows came again. The lifeless bear was so heavy that it was almost impossible to turn over. After much prying using the same leverage that I saw my uncles using to lift a totem pole in place, I finally retrieved the bear's hide for the longhouse wall. There I scraped it with tough clam shells that I found around the outside fire pits. Then I put the hide up on the wall, securing it with makeshift wooden pegs that I crammed in the spaces between the planks. It took several hours to secure the heavy hide as it kept falling back on me.

Already exhausted, I returned to the bear to
cut up and retrieve the meat. I made trip
after trip up the path as I took each piece of
meat to the smokehouse. There I threw the
meat over the rafters to dry. I even had to
bring in branches from the alder trees
growing in back of the smokehouse as
drying racks for the rest of the meat once the
rafters were full. There was so much food.

"Now Eagle and I don't have to worry," I
said aloud.

The rest of the night I carried the bear's
bones way up the beach, slipping on
the ever present seaweed, to the spot past
the rocks where I fished in the deep water. I
sank the bones there at the bottom of the
channel so no aroma would be left on the
ground that would invite more predators to
come around the village.

Finally, I got to call the night mine. I
lumbered off to the longhouse to sleep the
few hours that were left until dawn. I could
have slept in, too, if it hadn't been for
Eagle's screeching outside. It's amazing

how piercing an eagle's screech can be when you're trying to sleep. Eagle knew that the smokehouse was full of meat, and he was ready for his share. So I got up and fed the big bird, but then I wondered what happened to Smirk and Shylean. I saw her limping, but how badly was she hurt?

A week passed as I busied myself with keeping fires smoldering in the smokehouse to cure the bear meat. Suddenly, I heard a loud howling noise from the direction of the ocean. I quickly ran down the path to see Smirk coming out of the water with Shylean ever close behind. I could see that she was weak because she had lost many of her reddish-black, feather-shaped scales. These were no ordinary wolves, and they needed my special attention.

The two wolves gradually emerged from the water, Smirk walking slowly and Shylean limping as they headed over to lie by the rock where I had first noticed them. There I examined Shylean's wound as Smirk kept a close eye on me all the while. I hoped Smirk understood me when I told him that I was a carver. I could carve cedar scales that would match the ones Shylean lost in the bear fight to protect her wound. He seemed to trust me, so I ran to the longhouse to get my carving tool. I had fashioned it over the summer months to carve a totem that paid homage to the whales that lived in warmer waters yet traveled to Alaska each summer to eat abundant krill and plankton. It seemed as though the whales felt safe in the northern waters.

Similarly, I wanted Shylean to feel safe with me. I fashioned the feathered scale to the size of Smirk's that he lost a month ago. I made 28 of them out of red cedar, enough to cover the open area exposed to the salt water on Shylean's shoulder. I fitted each scale by slanting the back so that it would fit snugly to her body. I then secured them with small diameter baleen strips that slid through the hole at the top of each scale. I had formed the holes with an iron spike that I heated over the fire. Each piece of cedar looked like a scale, but two joined together looked liked a feather.

Then I crushed huckleberries that I had
gathered up on the trail to the village
carving center and mixed them with my own
saliva to make a red color. I also scooped
charred wood from the fire for the black
color and proceeded to dye the feathered
scales to match Shylean's. The process took
hours.

Proud of my work and hoping that my scales
would match, I ran back to the shore, where
to my delight I found Smirk and Shylean
waiting for me. Shylean timidly closed her
eyes as I began to feel my starting point to
secure the scales. I found it by the stouter
of scales that were much like the hard
copper shields my family used over the
generations. They were the ones kept by the
chief to give away at the grand potlatches. I
fitted each carved scale into place. When I
finished, I stood back to admire my work,
delighted that all the scales fit. I was also
very glad that Shylean remained still during
the "surgery." She now appeared good as
new. All in all, I was proud of my work as a
"wolf doctor."

Smirk snorted in my direction. I took that as a compliment. The three of us sat together looking out on the horizon; I was in the middle of my two wolf friends. My eyes became heavy as I began to let down from the day's events, and I soon fell asleep. I awoke the next morning to find myself wrapped in the warmth of Smirk and Shylean on the beach next to the knoll.

Chapter 6: Fog Woman

I watched Smirk and Shylean as they jumped off the knoll. They are making their way up the path, past the tribal house, toward the Fogwoman totem.

Seeing the Giant wolves lumber on the village path, Eagle swoops down to take a closer look. His talons grab onto the carving of Raven, who sit's highest on that totem pole. Eagle watches intently as the massive wolves, with the unusual red and black markings, make their way past the totem only to disappear into the dense forest once again.

I followed them until I saw my favorite friend sitting on top of Raven, his forever foe.

I decide to tell him another side of Raven since he has taken the time to sit on Ravens head.

Looking up at Eagle I begin my tale;

One day Raven, who had changed himself into a fisherman, set off in his canoe with two men from the village. As they began to paddle away from the bank, they set their sights on the deeper water past the rocks to the green-colored areas and then finally out to the deepest blue water where they could catch the King salmon, the biggest salmon of them all, which was full of the prized oil for cooking.

The three men were so intent on reaching the fishing grounds that at first they didn't see the dark grey clouds that were coming in rapidly from the southeast. If they had only looked up, they could have witnessed the denseness from the clouds reaching down to the ocean, a sure sign that it was already raining heavily there.

As soon as they reached the fishing grounds Raven got a strike! The King salmon ran with the hook and pulled the canoe out to sea. The big fish aggressively yanked on the hook and line; it even jumped and bared its side as it tried to shake loose. Raven held on tightly, not risking losing his prize fish. He was so excited in the struggle that he didn't see the storm rapidly approaching.

Then, the storm was upon them, drenching the trio as they tried to get the fish. They saw it jump again, this time close to the boat, but they knew it was only getting up its strength to pull them farther out to its own territory. When it jumped the second time, it showed them all of its glory of color: blue-green and purplish red on top with bright silver sides and black spots on its upper half and tail. Then they saw its black mouth with white teeth as it made its final bite through Raven's line.

That was it. The King salmon was gone. The men were definitely disappointed, but they soon became aware of the change in the weather, which gave them a lot more to worry about than losing a fish. The dense fog that had formed around the canoe was now as far as they could see. Not knowing where the salmon had pulled them, they sat to wait out the fog. They were afraid if they paddled that they would go even farther out to sea.

They waited for hours, but it seemed like days, when all at once Raven looked past his friends and saw an aberration of a tall, beautiful woman. The two other men turned around to follow Raven's stare. Her eyes were as dark as a mid-winter Ketchikan night. She wore the fog like a fur coat. She seemed to glide in the cloud when she moved.

Raven then said, We have been lost for a long time. Can you help us find shore?"

The mysterious young woman guided them to her village not far away.

When the four reached the village they were greeted at the water's edge.

Raven soon fell in love with Fogwoman. She was equally fond of him. It was not long before they decided to marry. They began preparing for the day.

   It was a celebration like no other; everyone in the village attended the ceremony. The elders said that it was a potlatch for all time. People danced to the rhythm of their hand-held drums. They sang their village songs.

They ate their supply of salmon and then feasted on the roasted deer. Little work was accomplished as the party lasted for five days. At its conclusion Raven noticed that they only had meat from the forest left in the smokehouse, yet he hungered for more salmon.

Fogwoman decided that she would help him get some salmon. She had special, magical powers, and she was about to put them to work. That morning, with the mist rising off of the water, she went down to the creek. Kneeling down on the moss-covered bank, she took off her cedar bark hat to use as a pail as she scooped up bright red salmon that were just starting to come upstream. When her hat was full, she returned to the village to give away her catch. Everyone was thankful, especially the children.

Fog Woman continued to provide salmon for the village over the course of a year or so. She also presented her husband with a baby daughter. This new village family was seemingly happy and content. All was not as it appeared, however.

The appearance of unusually large catches
of salmon left Raven curious and even a
little bit greedy; he wanted to know how
Fog Woman caught so many fish when even
the best fishermen weren't having any luck.
But she had vowed to the spirits not to
reveal this miracle, and she refused to tell
him. Raven would not be dissuaded. He let
his curiosity overwhelm him and followed
her to a large flat rock that was by the
mouth of the stream just at the level where it
flowed into the sea. He watched intently as
he saw her fill her hat again with salmon
from the deep pool by the rock.

Raven then confronted Fogwoman, "How
do you do this? I want to know the secret so
I can make a profit in the village."

She looked at him sadly, "I don't do this for
that reason; I do it to provide fish for all of
the families. Can't you see that they are
hungry."

Raven was beside himself. He became
angry with Fogwoman and wanted to learn

her secret so badly that he was unable to control his emotions " If you won't show me how to make these salmon appear then be gone!" he said before he could catch the misguided words.

With that the spell was broken and Fogwoman changed back into the dense mist and as such she immediately rolled out to sea. Raven stood there in the fog, his eyes searching back and forth across the water, but all he could see was more mist.

 She wasn't anywhere. Neither were the salmon.

Raven returned to village life and became quieter over the years. He rarely spoke, but when he did he spoke with more wisdom. He guided others who were in need.

In the end, Raven turned to touch the totem outside his tribal house one last time. He glanced up at the figure of himself at the top followed by Fog Woman, and their daughter, Creek Woman. It was this totem the master carver of the village had made for him.

Raven left his totem behind as he slowly went down the path to the flat rock, unaware that he was being followed by one of the young people of the village. When he reached the flat rock he climbed upon it with the help of his speechless cane. He stood facing the cool, calm ocean. Looking out to the horizon he humbly said, "I've learned humility. I've learned compassion. What else do I have to learn?"

Raven's chin fell to his chest. His silver hair fell over his face. Tears fell from his cheeks, splashing on the flat rock and reflecting the sunset like sparks from a fire. Suddenly he changed back into a large black bird and flew into the fog. Soon he was invisible.

Grandmother, who at the time was the young Creek Woman, strained to see her father on the flat rock, but the crystals of fog blurred her image. She also couldn't hear anything, not a sound, not a ripple, not even the calls of ravens or eagles. Then, from nowhere, came a swirling breeze that lifted the fog. The girl was sad and happy at the

same time when she saw her father's staff
lying on the flat rock next to a large basket
of salmon.

Fog Woman had come to take Raven home.

It was a long story, Eagle turned and flew
away.

Chapter 7: Sun and the Raven

"I often reminisced about the legends that
were told to me by my relatives. I enjoyed
watching my uncle and cousins carve. It
took Uncle all summer, starting with his
adze and then ending up with his straight
knife, as he made his mark upon the log and
transformed it into a story.

I look at Eagle in the silver bare tree above
me. I begin to tell him this legend that
inspired my Uncle to carve.

The story begins with a beautiful daughter
of the Chief of the Nass River. The chief
was a powerful man who at one time held
the sun captive from the sky. Because of his
action, the village people lived with
overcast skies and dark days. Some of the
young had yet to see the sun. Their eyes
and mouths were often as downcast as the
weather. They didn't smile or laugh much.
But the kind, generous princess had powers
of her own, and she was loved by all of the
people in the village. Her mere presence
gave them hope.

Raven had watched the princess from the

high hemlock trees since she was born. He
grew fonder of her as she matured. When
he saw that she had turned into a young
woman, Raven was enamored with her, but
he didn't think that he could gain her love
because her father didn't trust him. Chief
called Raven a "trickster." He didn't trust
the crafty bird. He had his guards watch the
skies to see if Raven was flying overhead.
He even had them scour the trees to see if
Raven was sitting on a branch in the forest.

Although he knew he was being watched,
Raven built up enough courage one day to
talk with the princess. He waited patiently
near her favorite stream until she came to
collect water. When she arrived, Raven
flew down and landed next to her. The
princess was only slightly startled before
she looked at Raven with her brown eyes
sparkling as if there were sunlight. Her hair
was so black and shiny that it had purple
streaks in the wind. Her skin was almost
golden. Raven was captivated by her looks.
He then spoke to the princess and told her
that he had been watching her most of her
life.

"I feel a great love for you, and I would like to be with you forever," he said.

"I've seen you watching me. You sound very kind, but my father would never allow me to marry you," The Princess admitted.

"Then can we at least spend the day together?" Raven asked.

Now the Princess nodded in agreement. Eagle who was sitting nearby threw his head back and nodded too. She made room for Raven to sit down beside her on the grass by the stream. Raven told stories to Princess that made her laugh. She liked Raven, but she was worried about her father's possible reactions to him. Chief did not like Raven because he could transform himself into many different things. Raven thought about turning himself into a human, but he wanted the chief to be able to know who he was. At first he didn't want to deceive the chief about his daughter.

But then Raven declared, "I will fly into the

air above the stream, turn myself into a hemlock needle, and then fall back into the water by you. When you see it, cup it into your hands and swallow it with the water."

The Princess motioned yes. She wondered what was going to happen as she watched Raven fly up above the stream. In an instant he was gone. In his place she saw a small hemlock needle drift slowly toward the water. When it floated right in front of her she brought it up with a handful of water and swallowed it. She waited, but nothing happened right away.

As she watched the ripples of the current she felt a slight jerk in her back. The princess reached back to see what the pain was, and to her surprise she felt feathers. A wing grew out of her back and wrapped around her. It was so warm. In the process Princess felt a love like never before. Raven hid himself before Princess returned to her father, who was unaware of what had occurred.

After many months the beautiful Princess

gave birth to a little boy. He grew quickly and no one noticed that he had some quirks about him, especially the feathers on his back. His grandfather loved this little boy. He would give his grandson everything except what was kept inside the bentwood box in the longhouse.

One day, when Chief was outside, the boy went over to the box and quickly opened its lid to release the sun back into the sky. This caused the boy to immediately transform back into his Raven form, from which he pushed the sun with all his might through the smoke hole.

Raven pushed the sun so hard that when it emerged on the other side, streaking back to its place in the sky, some of its rays had fallen off of it. These rays became the moon and the stars.

Through his power of transformation, Raven returned the sun, moon, and stars to their natural states. In the end he had deceived the chief, but he had also brought back joy and laughter to the village.

Chapter 8: Twilight

Inside the tribal house, I heard the north wind howling as if it were calling for the change of the season. The autumn nights were getting colder and colder, and I felt that I could sometimes smell winter lying in waiting. I often scanned the horizon, looking beyond the azure depths of the ocean, beyond the ever present grey and threatening skies, but I still had no sign of my family, Grandmother, or the villagers.

I knew that I had to gather more food. The rockfish supply was out there in the water, but getting to it had become more dangerous. The white-capped seas were never ending this time of year, making it nearly impossible to launch my small canoe. Even if I could, how long could I fish? Would I capsize in the icy channel and become part of the food chain for those creatures beneath the waves? The salmon had not returned to the stream near my village. I thought about checking the other streams, but they were so far away that I wouldn't be able to make it back by nightfall if I had armfuls of slippery fish to carry.

As I contemplated my plight, I noticed that Eagle, who normally sat near the opening of the smokehouse roof, was not there today. Instead, I heard his morning screeching call atop the hemlock tree. He bent his head backwards as he let out an ear-piercing cry. Oddly enough, there were many other eagles throughout the darkened forest. They were sitting atop the silver-grey, arrow-spiked cedar trees that stood out from the rest of the different shades of green hemlock and spruce.

The eagle clan seemed to be having a bird reunion or convention. They appeared to be talking amongst themselves and occasionally looking down at me as they conversed in their own secret eagle language. My friend, Eagle, then turned his head downward, and with a push from his mighty talons he began his spiral dive through the morning mist, making a stream through the air currents as he flew to me and landed on the rocks above the path that was close to where Smirk and Shylean had been recently.

I was familiar with his look. "So, you want some food," I said. He then gave me that intense look with his golden eyes. "I must tell you that today is the end of our rockfish supply. We have plenty of bear meat, but it'll be hard to survive the winter without the oils from the salmon." With that, I slowly and carefully tore the last piece of rockfish into two equal pieces, giving one to my feathered companion.

Throughout the day I completed my chores: I gathered firewood, inspected the bear meat, and carved on the cedar log. I hoped to eventually see the likeness of the whale figure that I was trying to create. This would be a base that was large enough to hold the carving that would stand on top of it. I planned to call it "Whale Song."

I had just bent down and examined the bright purple starfish stuck snugly between the barnacles of the rocks that jetted out from the bank when the beating of wings caught my attention. Eagle was flying toward me, and he had caught a salmon BY HIMSELF!

He opened up his talons and dropped the salmon in front of me. I hustled to catch it before it flipped back into the water; it was still powerful and looking for its lifeline. I secured my hands around its girth just as it began to eyeball the water a few feet away. Clutching Eagle's catch, I turned away from the salt water that was crashing on the rocks to see the other eagles now releasing their freshly caught salmon in front of the tribal house where I slept.

They dropped their salmon one by one, letting the fish fall to the earth where they flip-flopped under the weight of other fish dropped on top of them. One eagle flew down with its fish stuck in the toe of its talon. It was trying desperately to disengage a toe that was embedded in the backbone of an especially large salmon, one that seemed to be almost too big for the bird to carry. Then the talon came loose and the fish landed on top of the pile. It was a perfect shot!

The other eagles continued to circle

overhead, dropping their prey until the pile of silvery fish was so large that it reached up to the base of the carved eagle figure that held up the 42-foot totem pole in front of the tribal house. The figure of Raven with the sun in his mouth and the Eagle figure to the right of him silently watched over the salmon delivery.

Still clinging to Eagle's big salmon, I ran up to see the giant hill of salmon. My heart pounded, but it had nothing to do with fear. I was just so excited about the eagles' gifts of salmon. When I reached the pile of fish I fell to my knees. I was overwhelmed with gratitude. I had to take a moment and regain my normal breathing. I couldn't believe what I saw. I gazed up at the sky in thanks. I knew that I had witnessed a miracle! But then for a moment I became a little irritated and walked over to where Eagle was perched. I put my face to his beak and tried to speak sternly to him, but my words only came out as "friendly sarcasm."

"You knew how to do this? And you let us

go hungry on so many nights? You know, if
you had done this a little earlier it would
have been okay."

Eagle just grinned. He knew that he had
taught me a lesson. Because of him I had
learned how to be resourceful. I had learned
how to take care of myself and others. I had
learned how to survive.

I cleaned fish for several days. I smelled
like fish, but I was happy in spite of the
odor. When I finished the task there was a
mountain of salmon carcasses that was
almost as high as when I started. I would
give these "leftovers" back to the eagles in
payment for their generosity, plus a little
extra for their leader and my friend.

The bear meat had cured over several
months. Some of it stuck to the rafters, so I
pulled it off and put it in the old salt barrels
for later use. I had to make way for the
salmon to dry so it didn't spoil. It took me
all that day and night to gut the salmon and
cut off their heads for fish broth, the kind
that Auntie would make. She would also

throw in some dried seaweed that she had gathered out front, and the aroma would fill the tribal house. The smell would make everyone long for dinner.

I made numerous trips carrying the prized fish to the smokehouse without dropping a one. I filled the building to its rafters with the salmon, but I made sure to leave a large enough space for air to flow to cure the fish properly. Now, I had a smokehouse that was fuller than it had ever been.

Tonight I would sleep, not caring how many mice scurried about, but first I needed to go along the forest edge to gather the moss that grew on the rocks to stuff in the cracks of the house to keep out the freezing north wind. Once on the beach I stared out past the Tongass Narrows, past the little islands in the far distance, squinting to see if I could catch a glimpse of anything afloat further out. No one, no one, no one. It was going to be a long, long winter.

The moss was easy to find. It didn't matter whether I used wet or dry moss just as long as I could fill the cracks between the planks. All of it would dry eventually. A few of my favorite mice, now harboring out by Grandmother's woven blanket, watched as I stuffed the soft moss alongside the existing moss that had not blown out last winter. The biggest mouse kept its bulging eyes on me. Fortunately there was quite a bit of moss that had survived the wind, which showed that it had been put in with care the first time.

The planks underneath the carved Thunderbird needed extra care as that was where the round entryway used to be before the door was put in place on the southeast side. My nimble fingers slipped the crisp moss into the cracks. I marveled at the massive Thunderbird that was so named because people in my village found whale bones high up on the side of the mountain, far away from the sea. According to the villagers, the only way a whale could have gotten that far from the ocean was to have been carried by a monster bird.

The villagers once heard a thunderous cry

from the mountain, a cry so deep and so
loud that they thought it was thunder.
Following the cry were flashes of light.
They began to tell stories around the fires at
night and eventually created the myth of a
mighty Thunderbird so powerful that just
the beating of its wings produced thunder,
while its eyes flashed lightning bolts. They
also said the monster bird's talons were so
strong that it could carry a whale up to its
thunder chicks at the top of the mountain.

I let my back fall against the well-worn
grooves of the planked wall that was
touched by everyone in our village. The
wall had also supported all of those who had
traveled the seas to visit inside our tribal
house. Villagers and visitors had smoothed
the crevices with each touch, and the wall
became like the well-worn rail of my canoe.
The grooves were on the front of the tribal
house, as well. I went outside to look up at
the tallest totem in the village. It was
centered between the wall carvings of the
raven and the eagle. It stood over forty feet
tall. Auntie told me that it represents the
legend of the Sun and the Raven.

I like the carving in the middle of this massive totem because Raven went through an adventure similar to what I'm going through now. I remember it to go like this; One day Raven, who was alone in the world, came upon a gigantic clamshell sticking out of the sand. He could only see the top of it. Being the ever curious creature that he was, he hopped over to it and took a good look around. He began pecking, pecking, pecking at the sand surrounding the shell, kicking the fine pebbles away with his feet until the clamshell was sitting there exposed to his world. Examining the crack along the front side of the shell, Raven skillfully stuck his claw in the hole and started to pry it open. The process was harder than he thought it would be, but he was determined to get into the shell. In fact, he fought the shell for a long while until a squirt of salt water struck his beak. Knowing that he had made a crack in the opening, he fought even harder until he was pushed away from the shell with a force so mighty that he could not gather the strength to fly.

He tumbled backwards and watched from ground level as the gigantic clamshell opened. His slick, dark hair was ruffled now as he observed the first humans emerging from the shell. They were trying to hang on to the edges as they stepped to the ground below. Out came the humans, one by one, to begin their journey with Raven and all of the creatures of the earth.

I was amazed by that legend, but now it was getting late. I could see the light receding from the smoke hole above me. I needed to secure the sturdy staff once again against the door and head off to bed in the place of honor, next to the mice that had befriended me. All of us were in the chief's spot.

Much to my surprise, I awoke to flittering snowflakes falling straight down through the smoke hole to the flat cooking rocks below. It seemed too early for snow, but winter always came so fast. I felt unprepared for it, especially because my family and friends were still away.

I began my day with another surprise. I saw
wolf tracks outside the old wooden door. I
thought that I had heard some movement
last night, but I just worked it into my dream
about Smirk and Shylean fighting the bear.
Now there were wolf tracks! I hadn't seen
Smirk and Shylean for a very long time.
Who was going to help me with the invaders
this time?

I gathered what I needed from the
smokehouse, which was secure from the
wild animals lurking about. I took a hunk
of bear meat for myself and a piece of
salmon for Eagle, who was always there to
greet me in the morning. I threw his food on
top of the roof because of the chance that
another kind of predator was about. Then,
off I went down the snow-covered path to
gather some water from the creek in one of
the smaller, tightly-woven baskets. When I
returned I mustered up a crackling fire and
stayed inside most of the day, away from
any wolves or other predators that might
decide to make me their next meal.

That night, I heard animals snorting and

sniffing outside the door. Then I heard that plaintive cry:

"Owrrrrrooo, ow, ow, owrrrrrooo; rrrrrrr, ow, ow, owrrrrrooo."

Inside, the mice abandoned me and scattered under the floorboards in the chief's area, where I wished I could have hidden as well. I heard some scratching and reached down to grab a fat mouse. I missed the mouse, but my hand felt a leather strap that was connected to a pouch full of gun powder for the muskets that the men had taken with them.

I pulled out the pouch and inspected it. In some ways I was just like Raven; my curiosity drove me to investigate unknown things. I spilled some gunpowder on the rock by the fire. "Yikes," I screamed as the powder ignited and created a small explosion. Sparks flew around the pit area and smoke filled the tribal house. After that episode I thought that I probably needed to keep my curiosity in check.

I'd hoped to use the powder against the wolves, but I had no musket.

I searched my firewood stash for a suitable piece of wood that I could fashion into a "self-made musket." The hollow piece of poplar branch would do. It had a knothole at the base that could be used as a flash hole to ignite the powder.   It was the same idea that was used in my uncle's musket.

Luckily, I also had some dried salmon skins I'd been saving for pouches. I placed some skin inside the damp poplar so the powder wouldn't get wet.

It was now ready, so I began to pour in the black powder from the other pouch. I didn't know how much powder to use, so I used it all. I then placed a salmon skin on top of the powder to hold it securely in place.

Now I was ready to put in the small pebbles that I'd found around the fire. I figured they might work as "bullets." After putting several handfuls of pebbles on top of the salmon skin, I decided to put moss on top of the charge so nothing would rattle loose. "I think it's ready," I said nervously.

I propped up the homemade musket and
aimed it toward the door. I checked the
flash hole to make sure the powder was
exposed. I had seen my uncle do the same
with his musket. What came next was all
too unexpected. I thought that I would have
at least one more night to figure out how to
use my weapon. But there was no time for
practice.

I heard a large cracking sound like a
hemlock tree crashing to the ground with
the force of the wind. Then I looked at the
door, and again at the same spot where the
door had been. Two wolves that had just
broken down the door stood there looking at
me, but they weren't my friendly wolves,
Smirk and Shylean. The wolves' eyes still
glowed that eerie green glow as they
adjusted to the light. I reacted to them
quickly by jumping into the fire pit only
long enough to grab a branch full of fire,
which I swung around to place the fire right
over the powder hole of the wooden musket
aimed at the wolves.

"BOOM!"

The smoke, sparks and flame rolled out the door and up above through the smoke hole. I heard the wolves yelp, skid around, and high tail it out the door. The blast scared me, but luckily it scared the wolves even more. Then I grabbed another fire stick and tossed it out after them. My arms and legs were shaking with fright.

"Whew," I sighed. But then I heard a powerful snort in the corner behind me. It came from a third, larger wolf, crouched just under a wolf carving. The black hair on its back stuck up in the air. It was watching my every movement with its wild eyes, seemingly scared yet aggressive at the same time. Without thinking, I jumped back into the fire pit to grab another stick as the wolf rushed toward me. Its massive body kicked off from its powerful back legs to take the final leap up over the fire pit to the opposite side, landing so hard that the end of the floor board came up with a jolt. Then the wolf disappeared into the night.

I looked out after them only to see the first

two wolves rolling this way and that in the snow trying to get their scorched fur under control. The sparks were leaping into the snow just like the the wolves wanted to do to me.

With all my might I pushed the door back into place. I had had enough visitors for the night. This time I secured wedges of rocks along all of the sides of the door, locking myself in. I had to brace the door quickly as there were still little spark fires on the floor that also needed my attention.

 After about an hour, when the place was once again peaceful, the mice started to return. Still a little apprehensive about my plight, I said, "Thanks a lot fellas - for nothing. You were zero help in a wolf fight."

I had only the mice, Eagle, and myself to talk to all winter. I had plenty of time to think about the whale totem I had started to carve. When my family returned I'd ask the village carver to help me carve the eagle and a human to become part of the story where they welcomed the traveling whales back to the cool Alaskan waters for protection. And me, I hoped to welcome back my family in the same way.

Finally, my treacherous winter episodes were coming to an end. The alders began to get their reddish color of spring, but there weren't any leaf buds yet. They'd be coming soon. The southeast winds had stopped blowing so furiously, making it possible for the villagers to paddle the canoes back to the village. And back to me.

Each morning I'd fling open the old familiar door. Then I'd run the length of the path to the high rock and look far to the north where I last saw the village canoes disappear in a haze almost a year ago. Sometimes when I was feeling especially alone I'd watch from dawn to dusk for signs of canoes. Eagle flew in circles over my head as if he, too, were anxious for the villagers to return.

Two weeks passed before I spotted a log adrift. I kept my eyes focused on it during the next hour. There it was! There it was again! I saw the flash of a wet paddle as it caught the rays of the morning sun. But then I began to wonder out loud, "Wait a minute. What if this is a bunch of troublemakers from another village?" The elders had told me stories about what happened long ago when a warlike tribe from distant lands came to harm the village.

I knew that I couldn't protect the village, and the smokehouse with all its bounty would be lost. Crouching low by the rocks, I felt my heart racing as I watched the approaching humans. I wished I knew who was out there. I tried to remain motionless as I watched the long sweep of the paddles through the waves come ever closer.

Then I stood up straight. Then I jumped. Then I jumped and clapped and shouted with joy. I could see the likeness of Grandmother standing tall in the bow of the canoe as it approached. She was waving her arms even from that distance. I waved back. I jumped again and waved some more.

The entire village enveloped me on the shore. Grandmother gave me a big hug and then a bigger one. My aunts and uncles greeted me with smiles as they grabbed my arms and pulled me toward them. The children ran about as they jumped and yelled. Everyone was so glad to be home.

People began to ask me how I survived the winter. There was no food to eat. Did I catch fish? I didn't look skinny, so where did I find enough food to eat?

I told them about catching rockfish and about Smirk and Shylean. I told them about the bear fight. I told them about the eagles that had brought me so much salmon that I could feed the entire village. I told them everything that had happened to me as fast as I could get the words out of my mouth.

Then, as though he'd heard enough, Chief turned his back, and as he walked away he said, "I see you haven't learned in your year alone. Maybe you need another year."

Kegan, the adventuresome boy, came

running from the tribal house. His pants were torn from the journey, yet he didn't seem to mind. His face was full of surprise when he said, "There's a big bear in the house." He pointed toward the tribal house, and the other kids went running to see this enormous bear. The adults followed. Kegan proudly pointed to the bear on the wall as the others stood there in awe. They began to murmur. They looked at the bear and then at Eagle Boy. Many shook their heads in disbelief.

Chief went forward to the bear hide. He checked it out carefully for any holes that may have been caused by a spear, but he found no flaws on the bear other than some hair smashed around its neck. Chief then walked outside. He could not believe this young man that villagers had mockingly called "Eagle Boy" could bring down such a beast.

"Did you kill this bear?" he asked with suspicion in his voice.

"No, I did not." I said truthfully.

"Then who killed this bear. Who has entered our village?"

With that, three of my aunties came back with news from the smokehouse.
Almost in unison they said, "It's full of fish and bear!" Their excitement flowed from their lips.

Eagle Boy began to tell them again about Smirk and Shylean. He told them how the wolves had defended him against the bear while he was on the beach and how they had saved his life. He talked and talked about their friendship.

Samadhi, who was listening intently, came forward to let it be known that in future years she will be the storyteller. She would keep these legends alive. She held her cupped hand up to me and her eyes caught mine. As she opened her hand gently, I could see a fat little mouse crouched inside. "Is this one of your mice?" she asked.

"Yes, take good care of him because he took

good care of me," I said.

"Oh, I will. I just love him," Samadhi
shrieked with joy.

Chief was ready to say something when all
of sudden the canoes began bouncing right
off of the beach. He ran with the other
villagers to secure the vessels from this
random wave. As they approached the
wave-swept shore, they saw the head of a
beast with curled fins coming out of the
ocean depths. Half of its body rose and
showed itself to all who weren't running
back to the village for safety. It had a big
grin on its face. Next to it a smaller beast
smiled as they both looked at the crowd in
search of their companion.

There I was, making my way to them. I had
pushed my small canoe out when I first saw
the ripple from the water. I knew it was not
a white-capped wave coming in, but my
friends from the sea. I paddled right up to
Smirk, who sprayed me with a gush of hot
sea water from his snout. This time I liked
the shower. It was so good to see them

again.

I turned to the crowd on the beach. They
were now clapping and jumping up and
down. They were overcome with joy and
happiness for they knew that they were
seeing the elusive Sea Monster return to
their village once more. They decided to
turn their joy into a potlatch.

Smirk turned his head toward the open sea.
Shylean was ahead of him. They both
turned their heads back one last time. I
began to get emotional as I shouted, "Will
you return?" Smirk snorted what sounded
like "yes" into the air, and with that he and
his mate dove back into the sea. Their
whale-fluke shaped tails slipped gently into
the water behind them.

I paddled back to the villagers, who were
standing almost still on the shore. They
couldn't believe their eyes, yet they knew I
was real even if the creatures weren't. They
would be talking about Eagle Boy and the
Sea Wolves for all time.

As I parted my way through the crowd a
young girl of about three took hold of my
hand that was dripping with slime. She then
looked up at me hoping for more stories.
"One for Willow" she said. Again she
pleaded, "One for Willow."

For many seasons the stories would be told
around the tribal house fire. Each telling
would be more exuberant than the previous
one. As time passed, though, the villagers
were forced to pack up again and make the
journey north for better fishing and hunting.
One by one the smokehouse fires could no
longer be seen. No one was left to light
them. The tribe had to move, but this time
they took Eagle Boy with them.

Eagle Boy had become a man who was part
of a legend. His strength and courage was
revered by the tribe. He became a tribal
leader, and he and the chief's lovely
daughter, Ya'el, were united.

The village was eventually reclaimed by the
forest. The alders moved in first, followed
by the hemlock sprouts and the young cedar

trees. After 75 years the trees are now at
their magnificent girth of two feet. Eagles
and ravens remain, as do wolves, bears, and
mice.

"And that is only the beginning of the tales
of the potlatch," I said to my small
gathering. They got up from the rocks they
had been sitting on, shook my hand, and
started to disperse as I heard, "Thank you,
Mr. Talon." "Thanks for the stories."
"Thanks." "See you again, Mr. Talon."

Only Woody was reluctant to leave. He
clutched the stone mallet to his chest,
seemingly trying to hold the magic of my
stories in captivity just as the Chief of the
Nass held the Sun captive so many years
ago. Woody didn't want to let the tales go.
This made me wonder if he would become
today's Eagle Boy. I thought that he would.

I left my '37 truck on the bank after
launching the Alaskan Queen. Steam puffed
out from her smokestack as I guided her into
the afternoon mist of the Tongass Narrows.
Woody yelled from the shore, "Will you

ever see Smirk and Shylean again?" I
turned and smiled at him, thinking to
myself, maybe today, maybe today.

You can find the inner soul of a story by researching the books written during that time, about that time and shortly thereafter.

We thank these authors, from long ago, for providing us with the basis for Potlatch Legends.

Totem Tales, W.S. Phillips, 1896

Alaskana, Prof. James W. Bushrod, 1892

Alaska, Our Northern Wonderland, Frank G. Carpenter, 1925

The North Star, Sheldon Jackson, Dec. 1887 to Dec. 1892

Alaska, Marguerite Henry, 1943

Annual Report of the Board of Regents of the Smithsonian Institution, year ending June 30, 1888

Myths and Legends of British North America, Katherine B. Judson, 1917

Potlatch and Totem, W.M Halliday, 1935

Sea Monster

32' Chrysler, 37' Ford

Sea Woman

Whalesong

Tribal House

Inside the Tribal House

Thunderbird

Fogwoman

Woody

Eagle Boy Totem

Smoke House

Old Totem

Thunderbird & Whale, Skull

Canoe

Eagle with Salmon

Tribal House in Winter